C.C. BLAYNEY

AuthorHouse™ UK
1663 Liberty Drive
Bloomington, IN 47403 USA
www.authorhouse.co.uk
Phone: 0800.197.4150

© 2015 C.C. Blayney. All rights reserved.

No part of this book may be reproduced, stored in a retrieval system, or transmitted by any means without the written permission of the author.

Published by AuthorHouse 04/20/2015

ISBN: 978-1-5049-3767-2 (sc)
ISBN: 978-1-5049-3768-9 (e)

Print information available on the last page.

This book is printed on acid-free paper.

Because of the dynamic nature of the Internet, any web addresses or links contained in this book may have changed since publication and may no longer be valid. The views expressed in this work are solely those of the author and do not necessarily reflect the views of the publisher, and the publisher hereby disclaims any responsibility for them.

Thank you for the support of my family, especially Rob, and a big thankyou to "the Sudbury Girls".

Fred the Campervan

Fred could hear children's voices laughing and talking excitedly, getting nearer and nearer to the barn.

Molly sat up, looked around, and stretched her back, slightly annoyed that she had been woken from her nap.

All of a sudden, light streamed onto Fred. The old farmer had taken off the dusty old sheet that had been covering him while he had been in the barn. He had been in that barn for such a long time.

"Fantastic," said Rob, smiling at the old farmer. "This is just the camper we have been looking for. Can we buy him, please?"

Before Fred knew it, he was being lifted onto the back of Kevin's tow truck, feeling frightened. Was this to be his new family, and where was Molly, his best friend?

Charlie, Alfie and Rob sat in the front of the tow truck with Kevin, the mechanic.

"Are we going to keep the camper, Dad, and go on holiday in him?" Charlie asked, not quite believing that they really had Fred on the back.

Rob smiled. "Yes, Charlie, but he first needs to be checked over by Kevin and given an oil change and some news tyres, perhaps a new coat of paint and a clean inside too."

(Is that Molly behind the seat?)

A big smile spread over Fred's bumper. He was so happy to have a new family, *his family*, and start new adventures.

(Can you see Molly? Fred can't find her).

Molly had been Fred's best friend all that time he spent in the dark, smelly barn, not able to see what was making the scary noises, especially at night. Poor Fred.

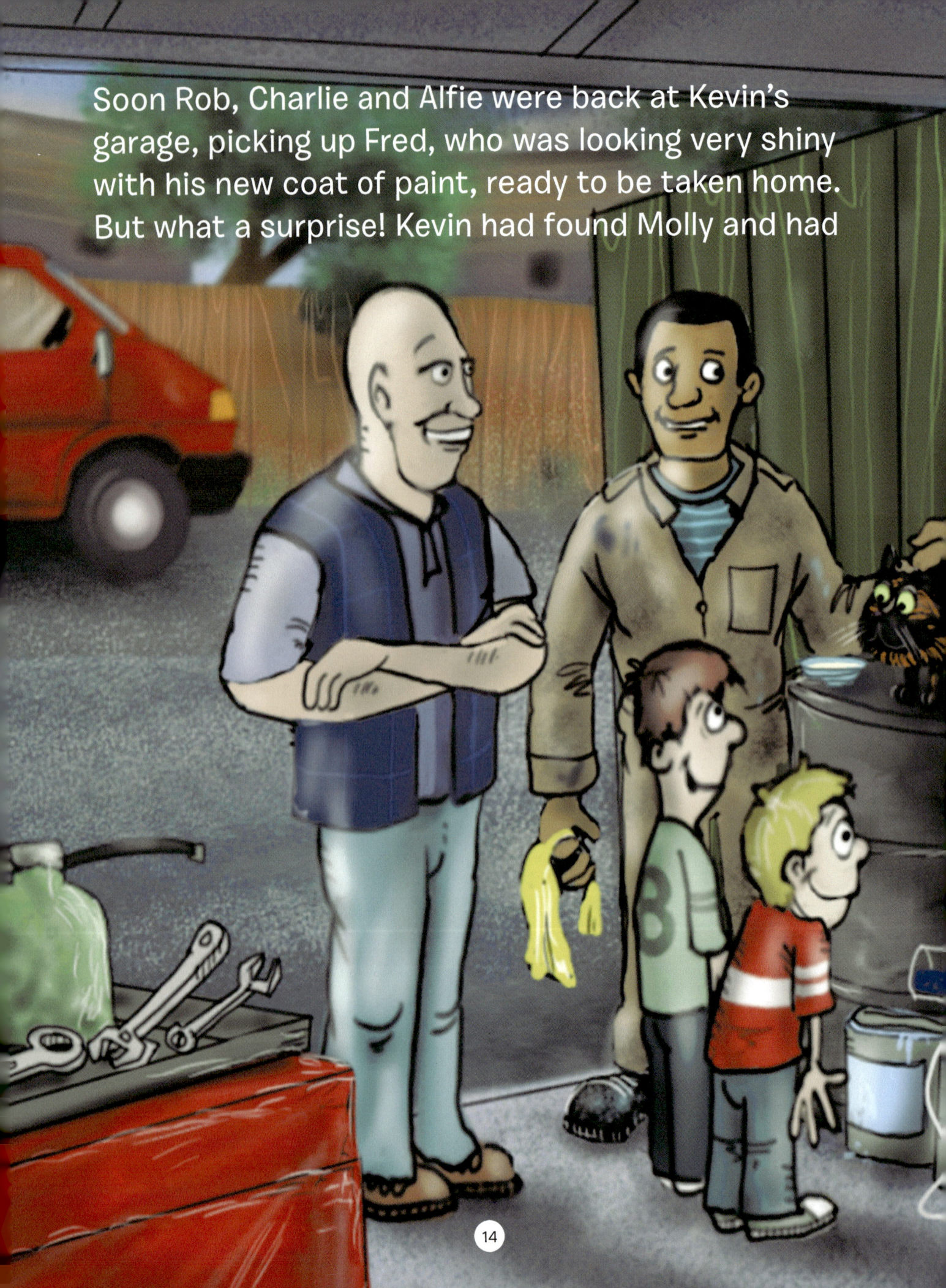

Soon Rob, Charlie and Alfie were back at Kevin's garage, picking up Fred, who was looking very shiny with his new coat of paint, ready to be taken home. But what a surprise! Kevin had found Molly and had

been looking after her, not sure where she had come from but knowing she wanted to stay with Fred. "Can we take her home, Dad, please?" asked Alfie.

Rob went to see the old farmer, who had been wondering where Molly, one of his best farm cats, had gone. He was happy to find out that she had chosen a new family and would be living with her friend Fred.

Fred then bumped and chugged to life as Rob, Charlie, and Alfie got in and Fred took *his* family home where Connie, Charlie and Alfie's mum, waited to see them, all excited to be starting new adventures together.

(But now where's Molly?)

COLOUR IN:

- FRED
- BAY
- SPLIT
- T 25
- BEETLE

How many Molly cats can you find in the garage? Find different tools, tents, and sleeping bags.

About the Author

I have struggled with dyslexia (mainly numbers or getting the right letters, but in the wrong order, most of my life!), but I love books. I especially loved reading to my children when they were young, looking at the lovely, colourful pictures and talking through what was going on in those pictures.

This is as important as reading the story, as it lets the children become involved, even before they can read.

I hope Fred and his adventures can help children of all abilities come to terms with reading, even if they have a learning issue, as there will be activities to do in all the books. Children can also follow along with Fred as he deals with common childhood issues along the way.

I have a camper van and enjoy going on my own adventures, meeting new friends, and seeing new places along the way. It's a great way to unwind and forget all the worries and stress of daily life.

About the Book

This is the first in a series of children's books with a campervan theme. The books will have coloured paper so children with dyslexia can read the book easier. Activities are included for children to help the time go quicker when they are travelling, whether they are travelling in a camper or a car. These are:

- Spot Molly the cat on each page.

- Colouring of the different cars and campers in the back.

- Pictures of all the different camper vans and VW cars they may see on the road at the front of every book, in bold colours.

- Crossing off the campers, cars, and lorries seen along the way.

- Recording the animals and buildings they pass on their journey.

- The books will cover different childhood situations (e.g. being frightened of the dark, friendship, going into hospital, visiting a garage for an oil leak, car boot sales, safari parks – with the different animals from other countries, camping, getting Fred's birth certificate from the factory in Germany, family issues, cooking, going to a camper show, taking a bride to her wedding, etc.)